Nod... ...rates

First published in the UK by HarperCollins Children's Books in 2009

3 5 7 9 10 8 6 4 2
ISBN: 978-0-00-731805-6

The HarperCollins website address is: www.harpercollins.co.uk

For further information on Noddy, please visit www.Noddy.com

Printed and bound in China

Noddy and the Pirates

HarperCollins *Children's Books*

Noddy and his friends were at the harbour.
Noddy was very excited because Whiz had a
special surprise for him.

Whiz was very excited too!
"You can open your eyes now, Noddy."

"Wow! Fantastic! A Jet Ski!"
Noddy cried in delight. "And in
my colours, too. Thank you."

Whiz was very pleased that
Noddy liked his present.

"Now I can go and visit my friends, the pirates," Noddy called, as he zoomed off across the water.

Whoosh! Splash! Whoosh!

"Hold on tight, Bumpy!" said Noddy, excitedly.

9

Just then, Noddy heard a splash.
It was his friends, the mermaids.

"What are you doing?" Noddy asked.

"We're diving for pretty pink pearls,"
the mermaids told him.

The mermaids had collected a lot of pearls.
"We've almost filled our treasure chest," they said, happily.

Noddy told the mermaids he was off to see the pirates.
They waved, as he sped off on his Jet Ski.

Soon, Noddy reached the pirate ship. "Ahoy there,
Noddy and a yo ho ho to Bumpy," the pirates called out.

"Come aboard
and play, arrr!"

The pirates welcomed Noddy and Bumpy
on board with a funny song and dance.

"I bet being a pirate is really good fun," said Noddy.

"Arrr! How would you and Bumpy like to be pirates
for the day?" the pirates asked.

"We'd love it!" Noddy cheered.

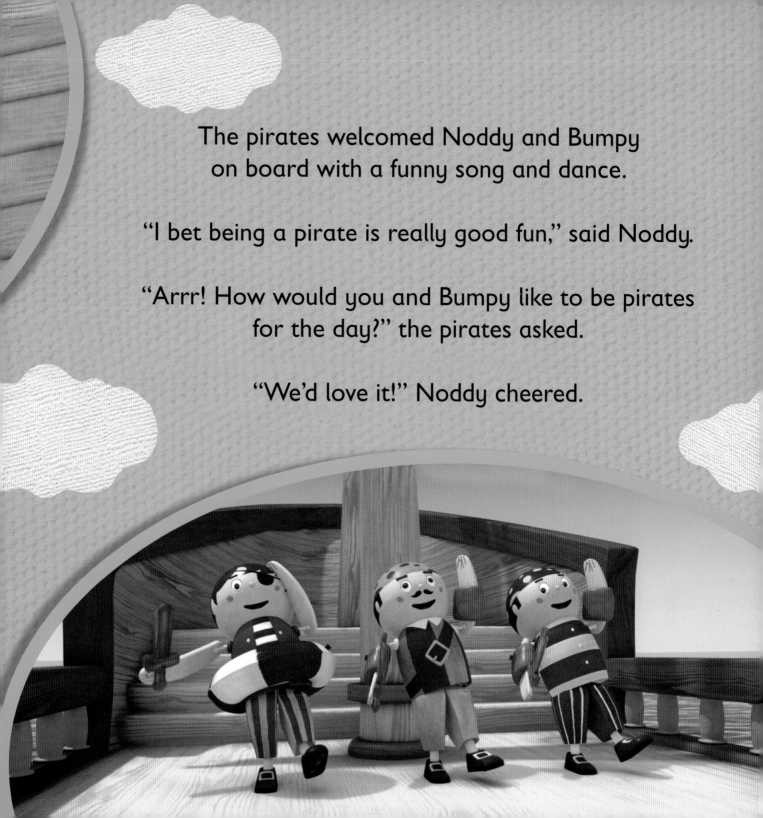

"What else do pirates do?"
asked Noddy.

"That's it really..." said the
pirates, looking confused.

Noddy realised he would
have to teach them
everything he knew!

"Pirates wear eye patches,
have parrots on their
shoulders and bury treasure,"
Noddy told them.

The pirates liked the sound
of treasure. They chorused,

"Yeah!"

14

Noddy and the pirates jumped
in a rowing boat and set off to
search for hidden treasure.

"Land
ahoy!"

Noddy cried,
as he spotted a tiny island
in the distance.

17

Noddy found some small stones
and showed them to the pirates.

"Look pirates, silver coins," he pretended.
"Let's get digging, mateys!"

With Bumpy's help, Noddy and the pirates
soon buried the silver coins.

"Noddy, how do pirates know where they've buried
their treasure?" the pirates asked.

"They draw treasure maps," said Noddy, holding one up
for the pirates to see. "X marks the spot."

"Let's bury some more treasure!"
the pirates cheered.

So Noddy and Bumpy ran off to collect some
big shells that looked like shiny gold plates.

20

But when Noddy and Bumpy
came back, the pirates were gone.
Noddy spotted them in the rowing boat.

"Where are they going?" Noddy wondered.
Then he saw a treasure chest on the shore.

"Oh no!" Noddy cried. "The mermaids' pearls!"

Noddy watched as the pirates picked up the treasure chest and carried it away.

"The pirates are going to bury the pearls, but how are we going to get off this island to stop them?" Noddy wondered.

Suddenly, Noddy had an idea.
They could use the big shell as a boat!

"Full speed ahead, Bumpy!"

Noddy cried, as they splashed through the
water towards the pirates.

23

But Noddy arrived too late,
the pirates had already buried
the treasure!

"You can't take other
people's things without
asking," Noddy explained.

"Sorry, Noddy, we were
just pirating around,"
the pirates said.

"Don't worry," Noddy told his
friends. "If we dig up the chest,
we can return it before the
mermaids know it's gone."

Everyone started digging as fast as they could.

"Ahoy, Noddy! I think the mermaids are coming back," shouted one of the pirates.

"Quick!" cried Noddy. "Here it is!"

Noddy and the pirates took hold of the treasure chest and pulled as hard as they could. "Heave ho!" they chorused.

The treasure chest flew out of the sand and landed on the shore, just as the mermaids arrived with more pearls.

"Now the treasure chest is full!" they said.

Everyone was happy. The pirates had learned how to be pirates, the mermaids had collected lots of treasure, and Noddy and Bumpy Dog had enjoyed lots and lots of fun!

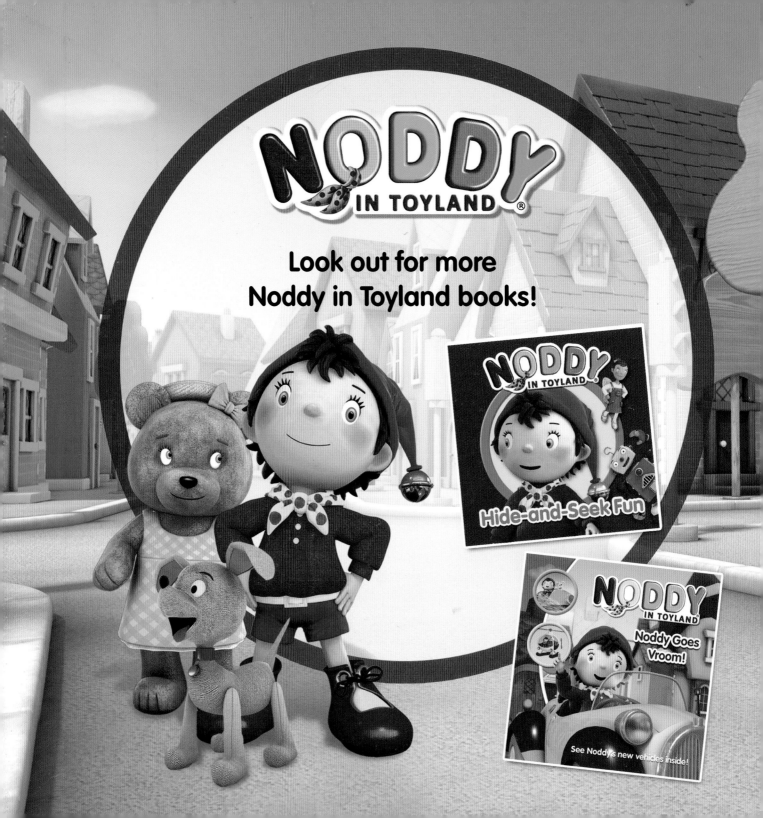